MOUSE VIEWS

WHAT THE CLASS PET SAW

WRITTEN AND
PHOTO-ILLUSTRATED
BY

BRUCE McMILLAN

Holiday House / New York

Someone left the mouse house open! Our class pet saw...

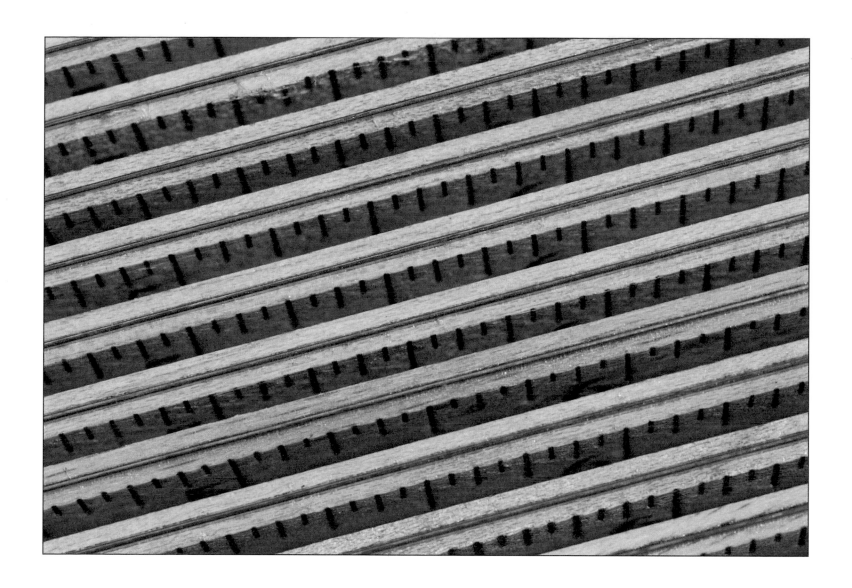

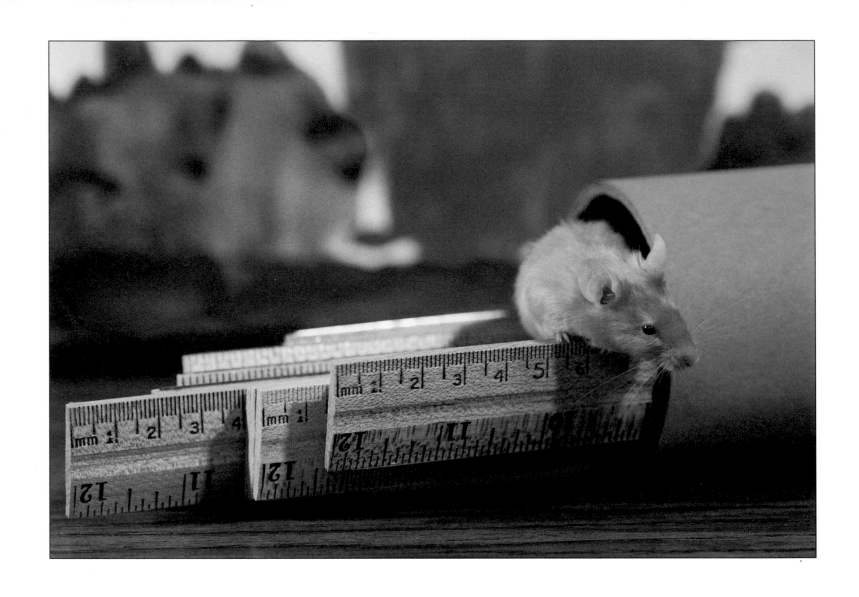

rulers,

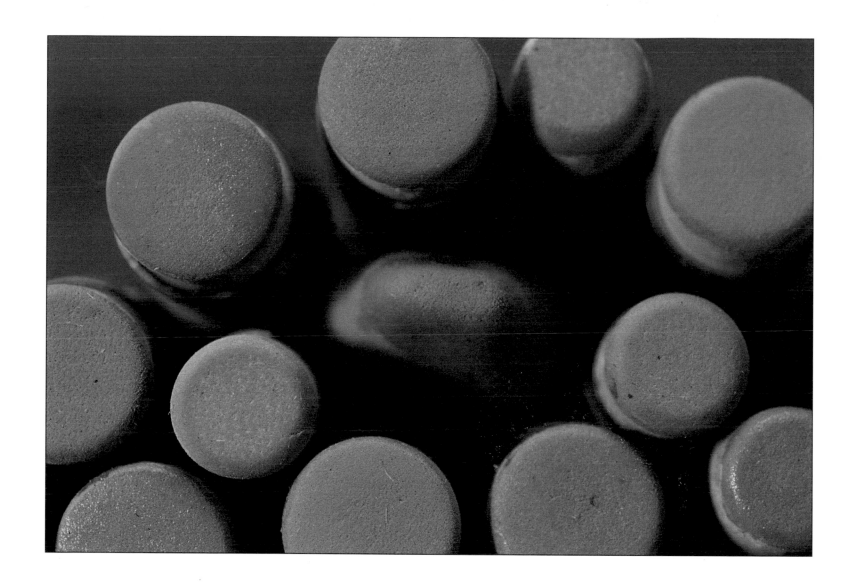

pencil erasers,

piano keys,

blocks,

lunch trays,

scissors,

paper,

paintbrushes,

computer keys,

books,

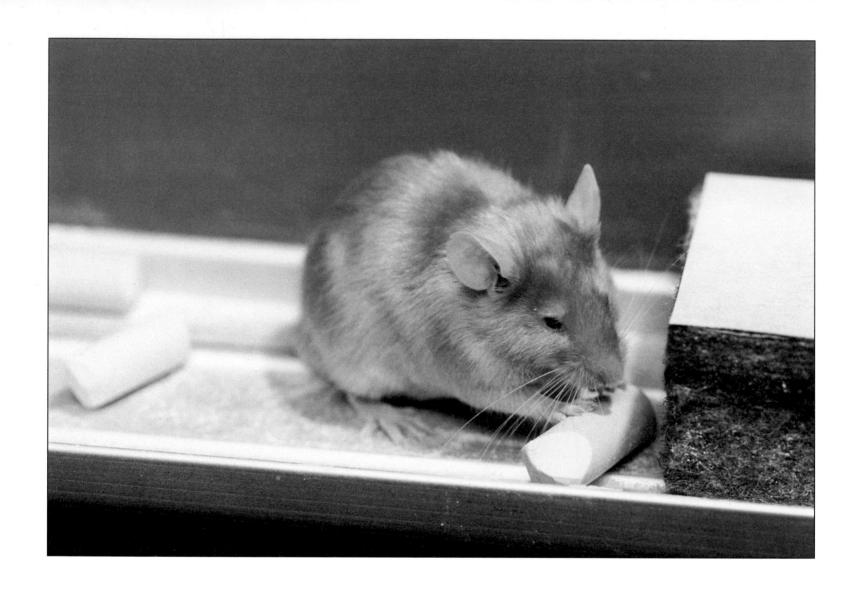

chalk,

crayons,

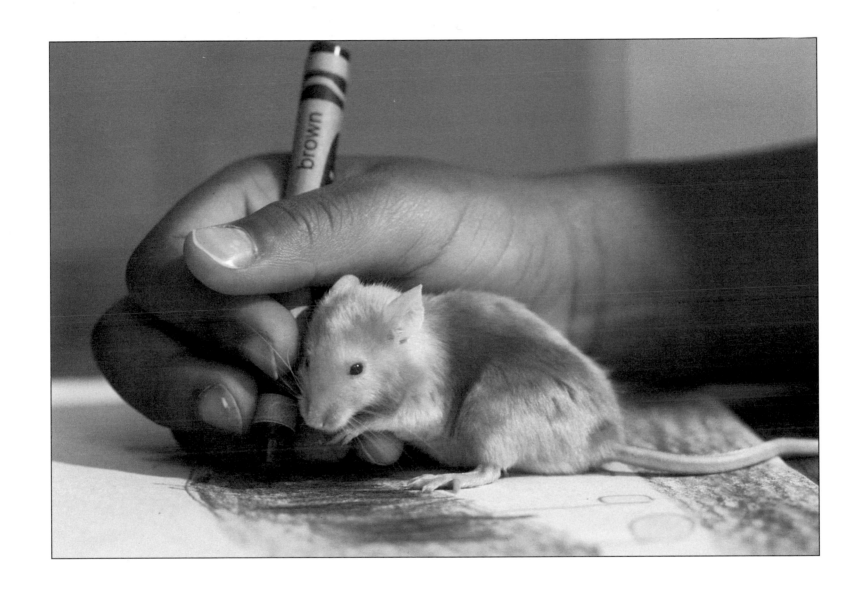

and

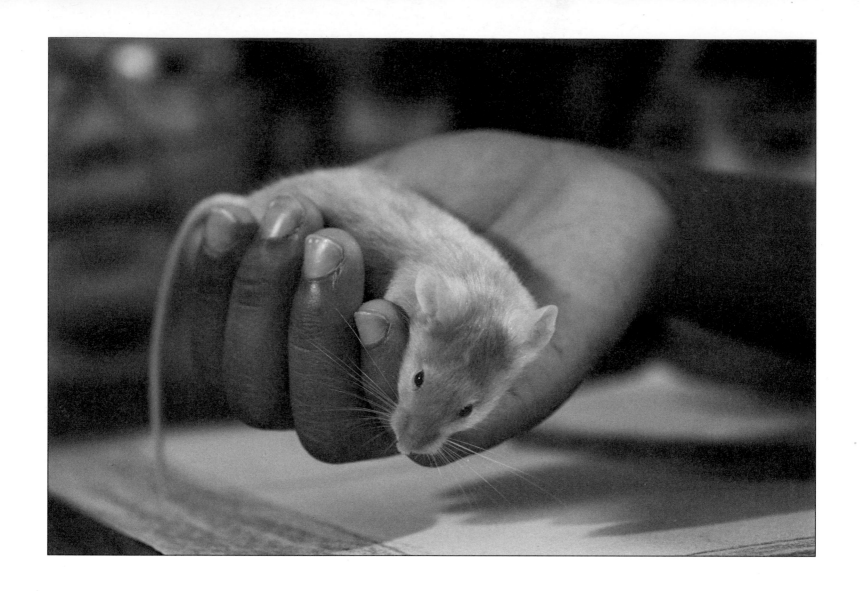

where the class pet went

School Map

start at A
the class pet's homeroom

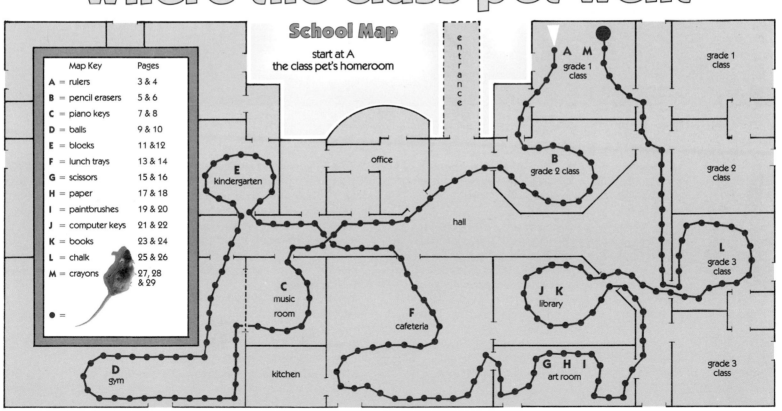

Map Key		Pages
A	= rulers	3 & 4
B	= pencil erasers	5 & 6
C	= piano keys	7 & 8
D	= balls	9 & 10
E	= blocks	11 & 12
F	= lunch trays	13 & 14
G	= scissors	15 & 16
H	= paper	17 & 18
I	= paintbrushes	19 & 20
J	= computer keys	21 & 22
K	= books	23 & 24
L	= chalk	25 & 26
M	= crayons	27, 28 & 29
●	=	

entrance

A M grade 1 class

grade 1 class

office

B grade 2 class

grade 2 class

E kindergarten

hall

L grade 3 class

C music room

F cafeteria

J K library

D gym

kitchen

G H I art room

grade 3 class

Library of Congress Cataloging-in-Publication Data
McMillan, Bruce. Mouse Views: What the class pet saw / written and
photo-illustrated by Bruce McMillan.   p.   cm.
Summary: Photographic puzzles follow an escaped pet mouse through
a school while depicting such common school items as scissors,
paper, books, and chalk. Readers are challenged to identify the
objects as seen from the mouse's point of view.   ISBN 0-8234-1008-0
[1. Mice—Fiction.   2. Schools—Fiction.   3. Visual perception.]   I. Title.
PZ7.M2278Wh   1993   92-25921   CIP   [E]—dc20
AC
ISBN 0-8234-1132-X (pbk.)

Design and map by Bruce McMillan
Text set in ITC Kabel Outline and Book
Color separations by Color Dot Graphics, Inc.
Printed on 80 lb. Warrenflo
First edition printed and bound by Horowitz / Rae
Copyright © 1993 by Bruce McMillan
All rights reserved
Printed in the United States of America

For Sheila

and

her teaching staff

This is a concept story about visual perception.   It's also a tale of a wandering mouse.   Preschoolers can see what "tools" await them at school. Elementary students can look at each "school tool" with a new visual perspective.   At the end of the story children can sharpen their map skills. Best of all, they can simply have fun.

When I speak at schools, I have lunch with the teachers.   Our conversations provide me with fresh perspectives on children's educational needs. Various teachers have pointed out a need for books to introduce map skills.   The floor plan map included on page 31 is in response to this suggestion.   I've also heard many amusing stories about class pets' escapes.

"Chase," the class pet, escaped at the Margaret Chase Smith School. When I first went to evaluate the school's appropriateness for the book, I was greeted by a sign over the entrance that read "Choose Us Bruce!"   It indicated the enthusiasm and gracious cooperation they would show me throughout the entire shooting.   Thank you, Principal Sheila Guiney, teachers, librarians, custodians, students, Jessica Massanari, and "Chase."

School: Margaret Chase Smith, Sanford, Maine
Mouse: "Margaret," "Chase," and "Smith," who are golden mice, and their cages were provided by me. "Chase," the golden mouse who starred in this story, now lives in Joanne LaNigra's first-grade class. His identical brother, "Smith," lives across the hall in Colleen Brady's first-grade class. Their brother, "Margaret," lives in another school.
Mouse Handler: Jessica Massanari
Students: As seen from left to right (page 30), Kenneth Wong Chi Yue, Sarah Pelletier, Matthew Faulkner, Jennifer Sarson, and "mouse-holding" Christopher Gamble
Artwork: By the students of Margaret Chase Smith School
Map: The floor plan shown is an altered approximation of the school's actual floor plan
Camera: Nikon F4 with 105 mm AF micro Nikkor, 55 mm AF micro Nikkor, and (page 31) 24 mm AF Nikkor with polarizing filter
Film: Kodachrome 64 Professional, processed by Kodalux
Lighting: Electronic Flash—one Nikon SB 24 with silver umbrella reflector plus two Sunpak 662 auto slaves with diffuser heads; for focusing, one Lowel DP quartz light balanced for daylight; and sunlight (page 31)